T0197602

Something New in Cloverville?

Written by
Janet Stuart

Illustrated by
Mary Connors

AuthorHouse™
1663 Liberty Drive
Bloomington, IN 47403
www.authorhouse.com
Phone: 833-262-8899

Because of the dynamic nature of the Internet, any web addresses or links contained in this book may have changed
since publication and may no longer be valid. The views expressed in this work are solely those of the author and do
not necessarily reflect the views of the publisher, and the publisher hereby disclaims any responsibility for them.

Any people depicted in stock imagery provided by Getty Images are models,
and such images are being used for illustrative purposes only.
Certain stock imagery © Getty Images.

This book is printed on acid-free paper.

ISBN: 978-1-4520-7701-7 (sc)
ISBN: 978-1-4817-1501-0 (e)

Library of Congress Control Number: 2010913692

Print information available on the last page.

Published by AuthorHouse 02/25/2022

authorHOUSE

Dedicated to my granddaughter, Chloe, who inspires me
to follow my dreams

Strolling slowly down the sidewalk, Eddie Hedgehog gazed toward the mountains. He was so lost in thought he almost tripped over Sophie Skunk who was sweeping in front of her store.

"Oh my – pardon me, Miss Sophie. I do apologize for not looking where I'm going," said Eddie.

"No problem," replied Sophie. "But I can tell something is on your mind. Are you thinking about our summer celebration?"

Looking startled, Eddie stuttered, "Yes, yes I am." Nervously looking around, he leaned in a little closer so no one could hear what he said. "Miss Sophie, as Mayor of our town, I want this celebration to be really special."

"But Eddie, everyone loves our summer celebration. All of the families come for the fun and food. How could it be any more special?"

"Well, Miss Sophie, I want something spectacular – something really different for the children. In fact, I have already ordered a special prize. I have to think of a super-duper new contest for such a wonderful prize!"

"That might be tough, Eddie. We already have a three-legged race, horseshoes, and a cow paddy throw. This is going to take some thinking. Come inside where it is cool."

Sophie and Eddie stepped into Sophie's store. In the middle of the room was a round table with huge, bright red tomatoes for sale. Eddie stopped suddenly causing Sophie to crash into his back. Turning quickly, Eddie shouted in Sophie's face. "I've got it! I know what my special event will be! We will have a tomato rolling contest!"

Bewildered, and still trying to catch her balance, Miss Sophie gasped, "What?"

"A tomato rolling contest! It's perfect! There is a hill at the edge of the event field. And you have all of these perfect, gorgeous tomatoes. Of course, there will have to be rules. You will help me list all of the rules, won't you?"

Sophie stood and thought for a minute. "I think it could actually work!" So they sat down together and wrote the rules for their new contest.

The next morning there was excitement in the air. In two more days, it would be Saturday – the day of Cloverville's Annual Summer Celebration. The citizens of the town were already preparing for all of the fun and games. Booths were being built for crafts and food. A fireworks display was being assembled. Colorful banners were strung from booth to booth. Mayor Eddie and Miss Sophie walked through the middle of all the activity to the edge of the event field. They stopped at the base of the only hill around for five miles. Eddie was carrying a wooden sign that he hammered into the ground right in front of the hill. Miss Sophie attached some colorful balloons that floated above the sign. Some of the noise around them quieted as everyone looked in their direction. This was new. No one had ever put a sign up at the hill. What was going on? A small crowd ambled over to read what the sign said.

Tomato Rolling Contest

Children only

Tomatoes at Miss Sophie's store (choose a good one!)

Bring a short tree branch

Contest starts at 6:00 p.m. Saturday

Grand Prize: Custom-built Skateboard

Excited whispering erupted all around. Parents started calling their children so they would know about the new event. Miss Sophie barely made it back to her store before she was flooded with customers who all wanted to buy tomatoes. The store was so crowded she had to move outside under a big shade tree. After hanging her sign on a low branch, Sophie set up her table and filled it with beautiful red tomatoes. All of the children gathered around the table to examine and compare the tomatoes. Mayor Eddie stopped by and gave his advice on choosing the perfect one. He and Miss Sophie traded amused looks as the children swamped him with questions about how the contest would work and what the skateboard looked like.

Finally the big day arrived. Among the excited children were Penny Porcupine, Willard Warthog, and Tubby Turtle. They gathered around the grand prize skateboard displayed on a table.

"Awesome!" breathed Willard.

"Radical!" squeaked Penny.

"Fast!" sighed Tubby.

"I can hardly wait until later today. Why did they have to put this contest last?" complained Willard.

"Because it's new and has the best prize," explained Penny. "We have to do the regular old stuff first. But I can wait because I'm going to win!"

"Ha, that skateboard isn't meant for a girl," sneered Willard. "My tomato is perfect. I know I will get down the hill first."

"You know," said Tubby, "no one said what the sticks are for and how the contest is judged."

"Guess we will just have to wait and see," smirked Penny. She and Willard ran off and left Tubby behind.

The day progressed and everyone had fun. Games were played and laughter filled the air. Food was everywhere and wonderful smells floated along with the wind. By six o'clock, everyone had played all of the games and stuffed their tummies with delicious food. Only the tomato rolling contest and fireworks were left. A crowd gathered at the base of the mountain. All of the children had their sticks and tomatoes. They anxiously awaited further directions.

Finally Mayor Eddie stepped forward. "Welcome to our new, special contest!" he boomed. "Are you ready to compete?" A yell went up from the crowd. "Ok, hang onto your tomatoes and sticks because we have to climb the hill!"

"Oh no," moaned Willard. "I didn't bring a bag. I guess I will carry my tomato on my tusk and my stick in my mouth. How will you manage, Penny?"

"I don't have a bag either. I can stick my tomato on my quills and carry my stick in my mouth, too. What about you, Tubby?"

Tubby looked up the hill and thought. "Well," he said, "I don't have tusks or quills. I guess I'll put the stick in my mouth and push the tomato up the hill with the stick." He slowly and carefully started up the tall hill as the others rushed on past.

Everyone was at the top of the hill except Tubby. Mayor Eddie spoke loudly so all could hear. "This is how the contest works. You have to roll your tomato down the hill using only the stick to guide it. You cannot use your feet or any other parts of your body. The stick has to be in your mouth. It does not matter who gets down the hill first. The tomato that has the least number of nicks, scrapes, and holes will win. Try to avoid the rocks! OK – get ready, set . . . Go!!!"

All contestants took off chasing their rolling tomatoes. Tubby barely got to the hilltop before he was knocked sideways by running bodies and waving sticks. With a sigh, he turned back around. He almost dropped his tree branch as he laughed at what he saw! Willard had slipped and was rolling down the hill along side of his tomato! Penny had pierced her tomato onto so many quills it was stuck and she couldn't get it off her back! Luckily Tubby's stick was forked on the end. He kept his tomato in between the forked branches and slowly started walking down the hill backwards. That way his tomato could not roll away from him. If he felt a rock with his toe, he kicked it away or went around it.

Everyone was down the hill except Tubby. The judges – Eddie and Sophie – were looking at all of the contestants' tomatoes. Most had holes in them with their seeds and juice dripping out. Willard had landed on his tomato smashing it flat and Penny's tomato was still stuck on her quills! As Eddie examined the last tomato on the ground, Tubby made it to the bottom of the hill. Eddie picked up Tubby's tomato and a big grin split Eddie's face. "As Mayor of Cloverville, I am proud to announce that Tubby Turtle is the Champion Tomato Roller! Come claim your skateboard!"

Eddie picked up Tubby under one arm and the skateboard under the other. He carried them both to the top of the hill. Eddie then placed Tubby on top of the skateboard where he posed for a picture. A cheer went up from the crowd and the fireworks started exploding in the night sky. Tubby lost his balance and flew down the hill on his new skateboard. What a "fast-tas-tic" way to end the summer celebration in Cloverville!